Activity Book

**Hello!
Welcome to Boo's
Activity Book.**

**There's lots to do –
matching, colouring,
spot the difference,
plus much more,
featuring Boo and all
his friends.**

Have fun!

2004 Universal Studios Publishing Rights, a division of Universal Studios
Licensing LLLP. Boo! and related characters are ™ trademarks and
copyright© Tell-Tale Productions Limited. Licensed by Universal Studios
Licensing LLLP. All Rights Reserved.
Published in 2004 by Egmont Books Limited, 239 Kensington High Street,
London W8 6SA
Printed in UK
ISBN 1-4052-1107-5

UNIVERSAL

Tell~tale

Draw a line between each pair of pictures that are the same.

**Colour in the picture of Boo
that is the odd one out.**

Find the shape Boo is hiding behind. Colour it in.

Help Laughing Duck find Stripy Cat by following the right line.

Colour in this picture of Bedroom Boo.

Boo plays with his toys in his bedroom. Match the right toy to its shadow.

Spot three differences between these toy rockets.

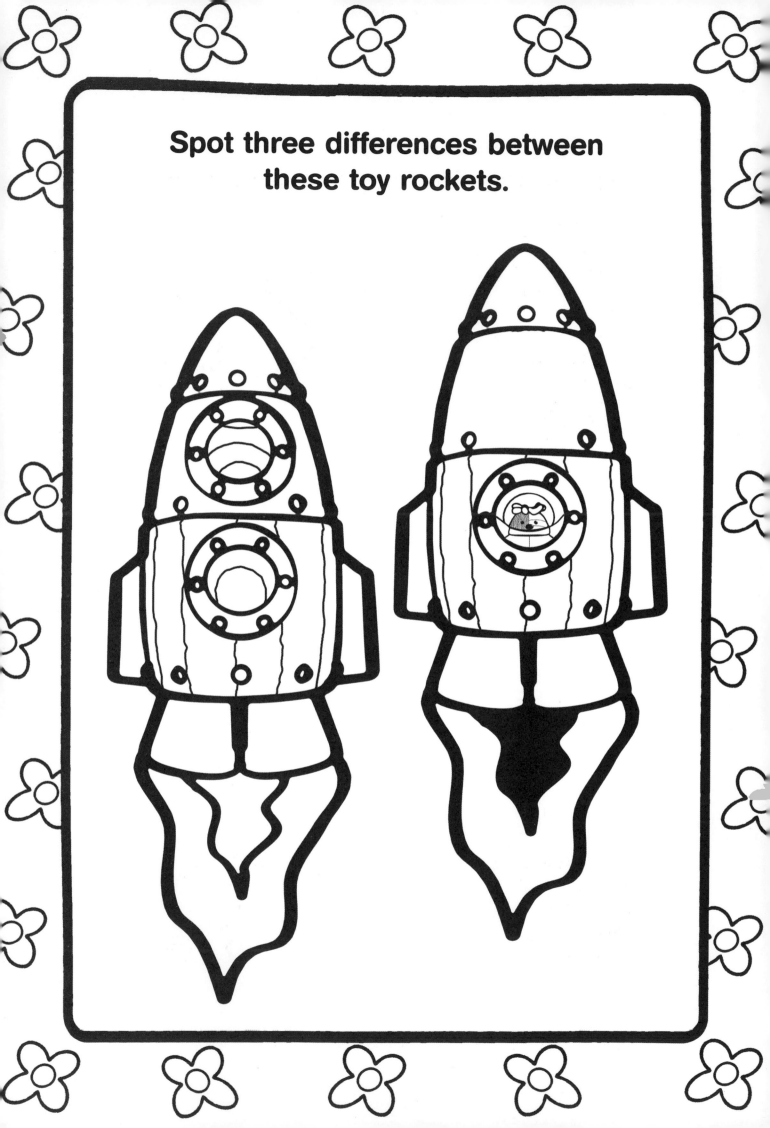

**Finish drawing Laughing Duck
wearing her space helmet.**

Boo is pretending to be a dinosaur! Help him find the flowers without bumping into any of the other dinosaurs.

Join the dots to meet Stomping Dipplodocus the dinosaur.

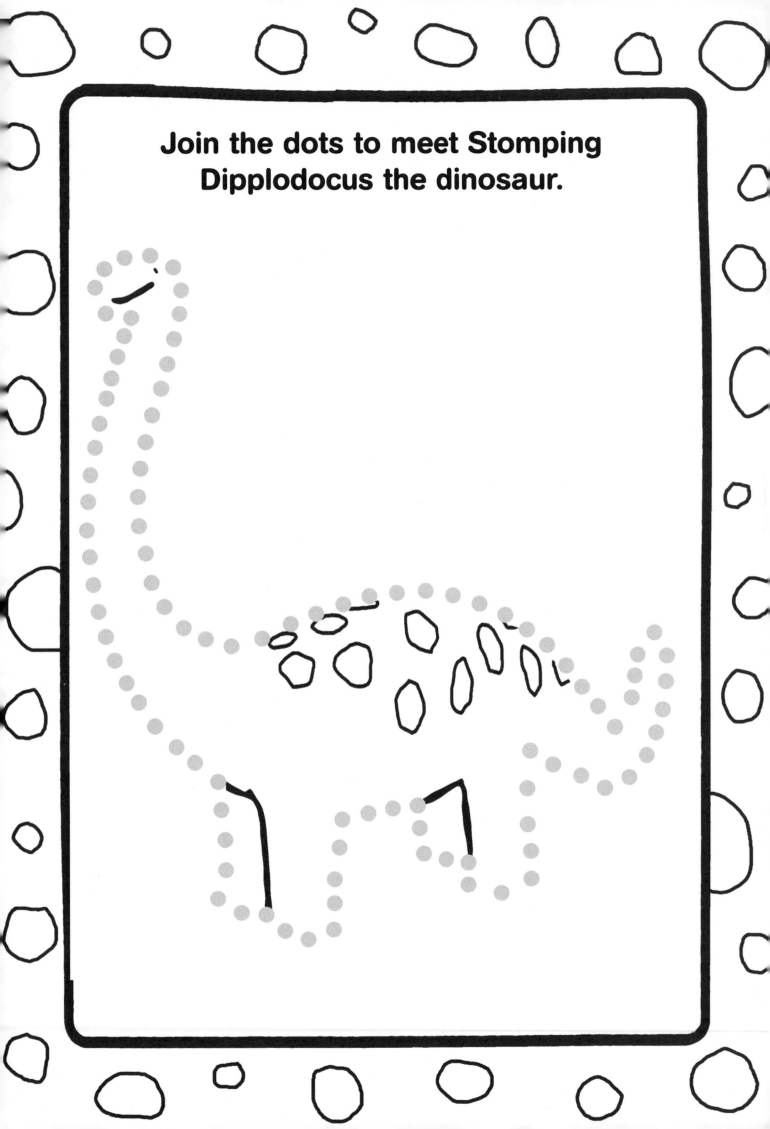

Colour in this picture of Kitchen Boo.

How many jars has Growling Tiger got? Circle the right number below.

1 2 3 4

Here are some things Boo has found in a rockpool. Draw a line between each pair of pictures that are the same.

Laughing Duck is wearing a snorkel to swim around the rockpool. Colour in the two pictures that are the same.

This is flying Ladybird. She lives in the forest. How many spots can you see on her back? Circle the right number below.

1 2 3 4

Spot three differences between these Ladybird Boos.

This is juggling clown from the circus. He has dropped a skittle. Can you find it for him by following the right line?

Find the shape that Clown Boo is hiding behind. Colour it in.

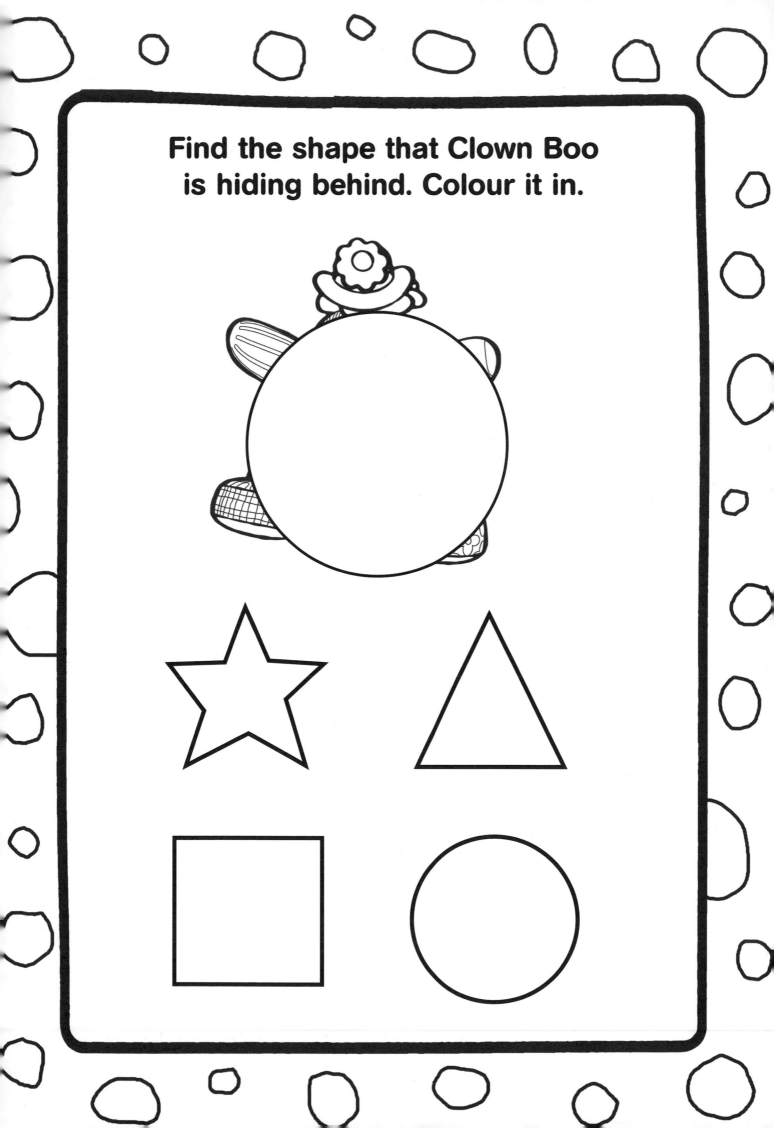

Finish drawing this picture of Bathtime Boo.

Join the dots to find out what is in Boo's bathroom.

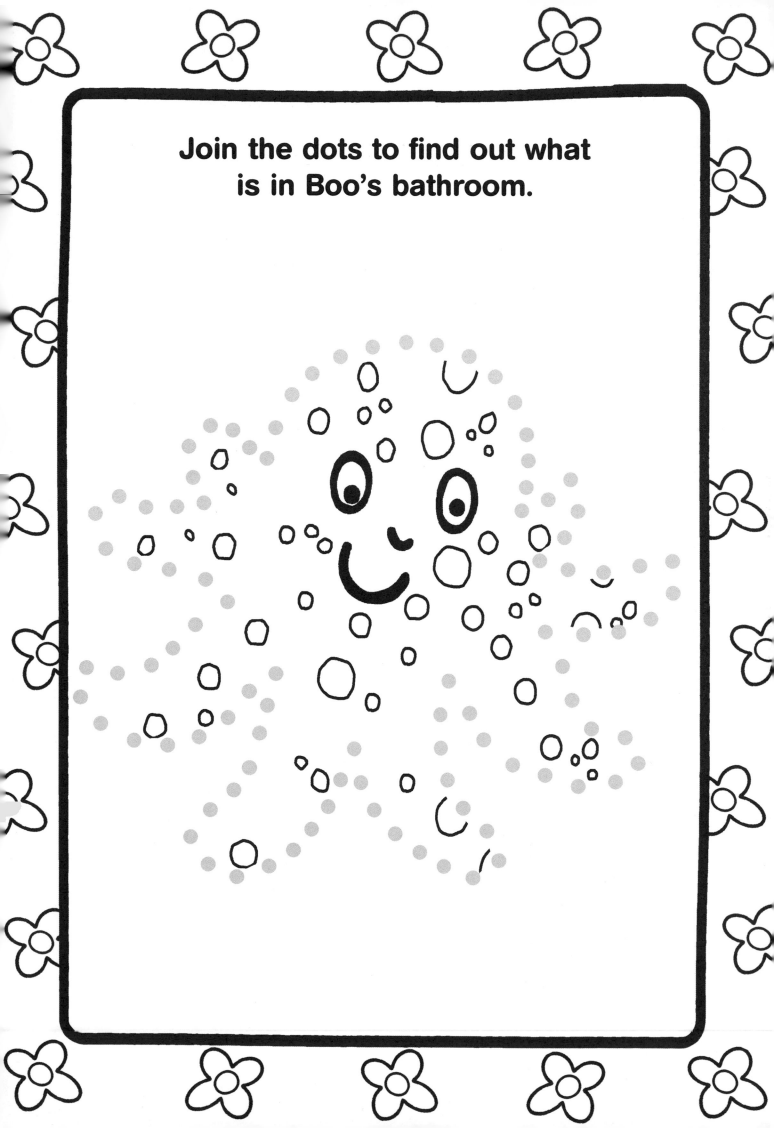

Match the right picture to its shadow.

Colour in this picture of Dancing Boo.

Have a good rest now, Boo!

Goodbye!